Dear Parents,

Welcome to the Scholastic Reader series. We have taken over 80 years of experience with teachers, parents, and children and put it into a program that is designed to match your child's interests and skills.

Level 1—Short sentences and stories made up of words kids can sound out using their phonics skills and words that are important to remember.

Level 2—Longer sentences and stories with words kids need to know and new "big" words that they will want to know.

Level 3—From sentences to paragraphs to longer stories, these books have large "chunks" of texts and are made up of a rich vocabulary.

Level 4—First chapter books with more words and fewer pictures.

It is important that children learn to read well enough to succeed in school and beyond. Here are ideas for reading this book with your child:

- Look at the book together. Encourage your child to read the title and make a prediction about the story.
- Read the book together. Encourage your child to sound out words when appropriate. When your child struggles, you can help by providing the word.
- Encourage your child to retell the story. This is a great way to check for comprehension.
- Have your child take the fluency test on the last page to check progress.

Scholastic Readers are designed to support your child's efforts to learn how to read at every age and every stage. Enjoy helping your child learn to read and love to read.

—**Francie Alexander**
Chief Education Officer
Scholastic Education

For Amy—who pulled through them all.

Copyright © 1995 by Nancy Hall, Inc.
Fluency activities copyright © 2003 Scholastic Inc.
All rights reserved. Published by Scholastic Inc.
SCHOLASTIC, CARTWHEEL BOOKS, and associated logos
are trademarks and/or registered trademarks of Scholastic Inc.

Library of Congress Cataloging-in-Publication Data is available.

ISBN: 0-439-59432-4

18 17 16 15 14   08 09 10 11 12 13/0
Printed in the U.S.A. 23 • First printing, September 1995

A Bad, Bad Day

by **Kirsten Hall**

Illustrated by **Laura Rader**

Scholastic Reader — Level 1

SCHOLASTIC INC.

New York   Toronto   London   Auckland   Sydney
Mexico City   New Delhi   Hong Kong   Buenos Aires

Hurry! Hurry! Out of bed!

Hurry!

Ouch, I hit my head!

Out my window, I see gray.

What a day.

A bad, bad day.

Hurry! Hurry!
I am late!

Where's my breakfast?

I can't wait.

I spilled my breakfast.

I can't fuss.

Hurry! Hurry!
There's the bus!

A bad, bad day.

We'll take the car!

What a day!

I got a star!

My Bad, Bad Day

Did you ever have a bad, bad day?

Tell about it.

What made it bad?

Rhyming Words

Rhyming words sound alike. The words **plus** and **bus** are rhyming words. For each word on the left, point to the rhyming word on the right.

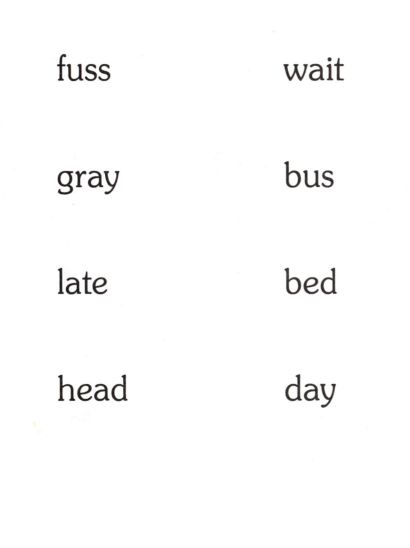

fuss	wait
gray	bus
late	bed
head	day

Feelings

People's faces can show what they are feeling. There are two faces next to each word below. Point to the face that goes with the word.

proud

sad

angry

surprised

What's Next?

Look at each picture. Tell what you think might happen next.

Opposites

Opposites are words that mean something completely different. **Big** and **little** are opposites.

Look at the words below. In each row, point to the word that means the opposite of the first word.

good   large   bad   silly

early   late   wrong   right

in   never   over   out

can   always   can't   funny

A Good, Good Day

Make up a story about a good, good day. Add as many good things as you can!

Answers

(My Bad, Bad Day)
>   Answers will vary.

(Rhyming Words)

fuss   wait
gray   bus
late   bed
head   day

fuss → bus
gray → day
late → wait
head → bed

(Feelings)

proud   sad   angry   surprised

(What's Next?)
>   The plates might fall and break.
>   The water in the sink might overflow.
>   The hamster might get out of the cage.

(Opposites)

good	large	(bad)	silly
early	(late)	wrong	right
in	never	over	(out)
can	always	(can't)	funny

(A Good, Good Day)
>   Answers will vary.